or,

THE EVIL AND CURE OF A PASSIONATE TEMPER

*

Written for the American Sunday-School Union

by

A deaf and dumb lady

Grace & Truth Books

Sand Springs, Oklahoma

The Evil and Cure of a Passionate Temper

ISBN# 1-58339-119-3
First printings, 1800's (date unknown)
Second printing, Triangle Press, 1995
Third printing, Grace & Truth Books, 2002

Cover design by Ben Gundersen

Grace & Truth Books
3406 Summit Boulevard
Sand Springs, Oklahoma   74063

Phone: 918 245 1500
www.graceandtruthbooks.com
email: gtbooksorders@cs.com

CONTENTS

"The heedless little Ellen came flying down the walk in her tricycle."

Part One

Rest for my soul I long to find
Savior of all! If mine Thou art
Give me Thy meek and lowly mind
And stamp Thy image on my heart.
~~William Cowper

"Now this is too bad! How dare you, Ellen, take my slate, when I had just done that puzzling sum, ready to show Miss Lee when she came? Now I have it all to do over again!" The excited girl rudely snatched the slate from the hands of her schoolmate, and by a single irritated movement erased the picture the child had been trying to copy.

"Oh, stop! stop! please, Grace, stop a moment! It is not your slate," cried the little girl, but it was too late. Grace had entirely rubbed out the drawing, and the child, bursting into tears, ran away, in spite of Grace's efforts to restrain her.

"How cross it is of you, Grace, to snatch things in that way. You are always flying into a passion, without waiting to see if there is any reason. That was my slate, and I lent it to Ellen. There is yours, just where you left it," said a young girl, removing a handkerchief that had concealed it.

3

"I am very sorry," said Grace, who, though passionate and very domineering, was not ill-natured. "I will go directly and draw another picture for Ellen, and I am sure that will make up for it."

"Perhaps it will to Ellen, Grace, but if it was me you had treated so, I should feel hurt still, though I would try not to show it."

"Well, what more can I do, Mary? I tell you I am sorry and am going to repair the mischief I have done as well as I can."

"And tomorrow, or perhaps even today, you will do something just as bad. I will tell you what to do, Grace: try to keep your temper."

"It is easy to say 'keep your temper,' Mary, but if you had as many things to try yours as I have to try mine, you would not reproach me so often for losing it."

"Why what have you to put up with that I have not?" asked Mary, "or rather, what have we either of us to bear? I cannot think what you want to make your life easier."

"I know we have a great many things to be thankful for," said Grace, who felt ashamed of the peevish tone in which she had spoken, "but somehow things always seem to go wrong with me. I am sure I wish with all my heart I had your easy temper, Mary — I wish I was amiable," said Grace, with a long, deep sigh.

Her sister made no reply. The same "easy temper" that enabled her to bear all the little trials and provocations that so irritated Grace, indisposed her to exert herself in arguing the point; and Grace, after waiting a few moments for a reply and receiving none, went off in search of Ellen, to whom she made the offer of drawing another picture. But Ellen also had her temper, and it now showed itself in a fit of sulkiness; she repelled all Grace's efforts for reconciliation until, weary of trying, Grace was forced to give up the point, exclaiming with even a deeper sigh than before, "Oh, I do wish I was amiable."

Mary, Grace, and Ellen Raymond were the children of a wealthy merchant; and fondly beloved and indulged as they were, it did indeed seem, as Mary had said, that they had no trouble or care that need ruffle their tempers or give cause for murmuring words. Mary was fifteen years old, and Grace thirteen, making both of them several years older than Ellen, but from the greater energy of her character and quickness of intellect, Grace nearly always took the lead, as if she were the eldest; and having firmer health and a more womanly appearance than Mary, every one at first supposed she was the eldest. She was of a free and generous spirit, warm-hearted and very affectionate in her manners and would have been greatly beloved, had not her violent temper and overbearing nature continually counteracted the effect and good impressions of her better qualities. Mary's tendency to yield had fostered these bad traits in Grace's character. Since Grace was never opposed by a person as firm and unyielding as herself, she had never learned to submit. Her father and mother were always too indulgent to all their children and never thought of offering anything more than a mild reproof or rebuke to her fits of pride and passion, and even these were always silenced by a profession of repentance and a promise of amendment, which were never kept more than a day or two. And all the household, from the lowest servant up to her sisters and Miss Lee, their governess, were daily compelled to submit to her will for the sake of peace and quietness.

It must not be supposed, however, that Grace herself was blind to the defects in her character. She was too discriminating not to perceive and had too keen a sense of what is excellent and admirable not to lament over and resolve against her many failings. Yes, again and again she determined "she would be good" and "she would be amiable." But there was no apparent change. Poor Grace! She resolved in her own strength. She desired to be good, to gain the praise of her family and friends! — and what a wound it was to her, that she failed!

Mr. and Mrs. Raymond were not professedly religious. They respected the Sabbath; they went regularly to church when it did not rain; and Mr. Raymond punctually required the attendance of all his children and taught them to show respect for the ordinances of religion, both by precept and example. But he never told them how these privileges ought to be improved. He never seemed to value or delight in them himself, and it is vain to expect that the duties of religion will be otherwise than irksome when performed only from a sense of duty and necessity, and not as the free offerings of devoted love to the Saviour. Thus, although Grace had been well-taught in the mere outward forms of religion, she had never learned to look on it as something that must enter into and take possession of the heart and be acted out in the life. She never considered that it must be an abiding principle; and though she felt there was much in her disposition that required improvement, she never looked on religion as the way to bring this change to pass; to her, religion seemed a thing apart from every-day life.

The church which the family attended was blessed with a truly pious and conscientious pastor, so that from her earliest childhood Grace had heard the doctrine of the entire alienation of the human heart from God's holiness and the necessity of a thorough spiritual change, taught in a plain and forcible manner. But she had never applied these doctrines to herself. She knew that she possessed some, at least, of what the world called amiable qualities, and she never dreamed that even these were perverted and wrongly used, because not used for God's glory. She was sufficiently advanced in mind to appreciate the truths of the sermons she heard. But if anyone would apply the sermon to herself, and suggest that she had need of repentance and a change of heart, the pride of her fallen nature would rise indignantly. She had been heard to exclaim, "I know I am sometimes passionate and overbearing, but I am sure I have never been so terribly wicked. I am sure there is some good in me!" Like most persons, Grace did not know herself.

Mary possessed a far less marked and decided character. Of a naturally mild and yielding disposition, she could, without much effort, be submissive and obedient. She was not lazy, but rarely exerted herself, due to her rather delicate health. This always made her unwilling to give herself more trouble than was absolutely necessary; and, far inferior to Grace, both in abilities and perseverance, she never imagined that she could influence her headstrong sister. She was truly gentle, but with so little energy and withal so quiet, even the good example Mary set scarcely attracted notice and was of little influence because it evidently cost her nothing to set it. She was not without faults, however, and of these the most prominent was a steady feeling of self-satisfaction. Indeed, she might be called self-righteous. She saw Grace as always saying or doing something wrong; always offending one or another member of the family, while she, in her steady, quiet course, was always on good terms with all and was everybody's favorite. Grace knew she had some faults; but Mary supposed she was never chargeable with anything really wrong.

The little Ellen, her father's darling, and her mother's pet, was to everyone else, that most disagreeable torment — she was *the spoiled child.* Possessing much of Grace's swiftness of mind and some of Mary's quiet submission, she might, under judicious training, have become a happy and useful woman, but in the unrestrained indulgence she enjoyed, there was the greatest danger of her becoming a very different character. The unqualified praise and flattery bestowed on her made her quite vain, and the overbearing temper of Grace, from which even her mother could not always shield her, excited fits of sullenness, which she would show to all indiscriminately, whether the object of her displeasure had offended her or not.

With all her angry feelings excited by little Ellen's stubborn resistance of her efforts at reconciliation, Grace returned to the school-room where she had left Mary, and here a fresh cause of irritation awaited her. Miss Lee, who had meanwhile examined her sum, pronounced it wholly incorrect, and so Grace found that the persevering labour of more than an hour had only resulted in disappointment.

"I declare, this is too provoking to bear," she exclaimed, as her teacher handed her the slate with a line drawn through every figure. "I never tried more earnestly to do a thing well than that! And now to fail!" And with a quick movement she threw the slate on the table again.

Miss Lee coloured. She had often deeply felt the disrespect with which Grace treated her, and it required all the patience of a Christian to induce her to bear with it calmly; but even with this, she would not have felt it her duty to continue in a situation where she was so treated, had not her generous salary been necessary for the support of her needy mother. She knew if she left Mr. Raymond's, she could easily get a more comfortable home, for she had superior abilities; but few could afford to pay the sum which she received for her present duties. And though it was not without an effort and some secret bitter tears, she firmly adhered to it, and never allowed her family to know the sacrifice at which much of their comfort was purchased. Yet still, though she could repress the sharp reproof which she knew would only induce Grace's angry reply, she could not altogether conceal her wounded feelings, and that silent look or tear sometimes softened even Grace. However, on this occasion, Grace was too much out of temper to even notice the expression of grief in the face of her governess.

Knowing by experience that it was useless to attempt to control her in her present mood, Miss Lee could only wait until the storm should subside before she attempted to insist on another trial of the difficult sum. She had not to wait long. Grace was too proud and too determined to allow herself even to seem overcome by a difficulty, and too active to sit doing nothing; so in less than a quarter of an hour the slate was taken up again, and after a short season of resolute application, she returned it to Miss Lee with the triumphant assurance that she was right. So it proved to be, and Grace recovered her good mood sufficiently, to make a half-apology for her rude behaviour, saying that she "did not mean any thing," and that Ellen had made her angry.

"But I understood that you first provoked her," said Miss Lee; "and besides, even if it were as you say, is it right to punish me with your displeasure with her?"

The gentle tone with which this was uttered and the look that accompanied it entirely subdued Grace, and, blushing deeply, she entreated pardon for her rudeness; so, truly does the "soft answer turn away wrath."

Grace's sorrow did not this time evaporate so quickly as usual. The marked contrast between her own behaviour under provocation and that of Miss Lee, struck her, and made her thoughtful; and the more she dwelt on it the more she longed to possess the meekness and patience she so much admired, and which she saw were not inconsistent with true dignity, for, (she thought within herself) "I never do feel so much respect for Miss Lee as when we have had a little tiff, and she had shown me how patiently

11

she can bear what would make me very angry." And once more, for perhaps the hundredth time, she resolved to imitate it, to govern her temper and to "be amiable."

It happened that for nearly a week everything went on smoothly for Grace. Nothing occurred to ruffle her temper, and, well pleased with herself, for a short time she felt secure that she was near to gaining a victory over it. She never considered that her temper had not been tested during all this time, and with her feeling of security she relaxed her watchfulness, and as she became more careless, little by little she became more irritable. Then, instead of taking warning by her weakness and making new and more resolute efforts to govern herself, she felt vexed and impatient at it. This feeling of vexation with self was accompanied by a still greater ill-humour with others than usual, and so disagreeable did she contrive to make herself that even the placid Mary was both afraid and unwilling to make her a companion. Grace, avoided by her sisters and thoroughly dissatisfied with herself, was seriously unhappy. Perfectly aware of the source of her misery, and yet ignorant how to remedy it, she became day by day more moody, which disheartened her from even attempting a fresh reformation of her ways.

Miss Lee saw and pitied the state of Grace's mind, as she had witnessed with interest the failure of Grace's attempt; but as Grace had never confided in her on this subject, she did not feel at liberty to offer her advice unasked. Thus Miss Lee had to content herself in earnest prayer for Grace, watching for an opportunity to speak, without so much risk of giving offence.

Miss Lee was a genuine Christian, and so it was no small trial to her to be living among those who professed no love for God and showed no zeal for His service. Beyond a mere heartless attention to the outward forms, on the Sabbath going to church, and, perhaps, reading a chapter of the Bible at home, there was nothing to lead anyone to suppose that one member of the family ever thought of God or of the world to come. Mr. Raymond was an honourable man and would have scorned any offence against what he regarded as the laws of morality, however small it might be, but he would have condemned it, not because it offended God, but because it was held in contempt by man. Provided his own character and that of his family could stand the scrutiny of the world, he was satisfied; and if he ever gave a thought to the time when they would be judged by Him who "trieth the heart", he quieted himself by supposing "they were as good as other people and did no harm to anyone, and what more could be required of them?"

With these feelings, he naturally regarded as fanatics or hypocrites those who professed to make religion their first and chief concern. He thought it should be confined to Sunday and the church, and that it was mere talk to profess to make it a subject of every-day conversation or to pretend to its influencing the actions of every-day life.

Miss Lee was well aware of all this. At the time he hired her as the teacher of his children, Mr. Raymond had hinted, as plainly and politely as he could, his desire that she would not attempt to tinge them with her "peculiar religious opinions" or make them "too righteous"; and, although he did not prohibit conversation on religious subjects, she plainly saw he meant her so to take it. She was not, however, to be restrained by such hints from speaking to her young charge directly on the subject, if opportunity offered, but it had been studiously avoided by Mary and Grace. Even little Ellen seemed unwilling to hear her, and she had too much sense and prudence to force the subject upon their attention. Still more earnestly, however, did she endeavour, by prayer and example, to do them all the good in her power. Even though she had been nearly a year with them without having made any apparent progress in this respect, she still steadily pursued her way, satisfied to do her duty and leave the result to God, believing her efforts would yet produce fruit.

"Come, Mary, let us play chickens," said Grace one afternoon; "I know you have learned all your lessons, and I have just done with mine."

"I would be quite willing to play, Grace," replied her sister, "but when you lose, you become so angry, it is quite unpleasant; and if I do not try my very best to win, you get into a temper with me and say I treat you like a child and do not take any interest in the game. So, I had rather not play."

"Then let it alone," said Grace, tartly, "only the next time you wish to play, do not call me rude for it."

"I never do call you rude or ill-natured unless you provoke me to it, Grace," said Mary; "but as you seem determined to quarrel, you must find someone else to quarrel with, for I shall go and sit with mother"; and taking her books and workbox, Mary left the room, and Grace remained alone.

Angry with Mary for her refusal, and not the less so because she knew there was good reason for it, Grace sat and brooded over her vexations. "I wonder," she thought, "why I am so much more unhappy than my sisters. I am sure if I am a little quicker in my temper than they are, I cannot help it, and it ought to make them more forbearing. I think they must see I have tried again and again to cure it, and if I cannot, why do they blame me? It is unkind and unjust, and if they loved me, they would not treat me so" – and thus thinking, she fell into the common error of blaming her unhappiness on others, rather than on the "evil heart within"; and working herself up to the belief that she was judged with severity and unfairness, she gave way to a fit of passionate and grievous tears.

With her face buried in her handkerchief, leaning on the arm of her chair, she was weeping without restraint when the light touch of a soft hand on her shoulder came. "What is the matter, my dear Grace?," she heard; and looking up, met the mild eyes of Miss Lee fixed on her with so pitying and affectionate an expression as quite to disarm her of all the pride and resentment in her heart.

"Grace, my dear Grace, why are you so unhappy?" repeated Miss Lee. "Can I do nothing to relieve you? Let me share, if I cannot lighten, your trouble," and drawing her chair beside Grace, she seated herself as she clasped the half-reluctant hand of her companion.

"It is nothing! I was out of spirits and felt dull," said Grace, blushing, for she was ashamed of the real cause of her tears.

"My dear girl, do you know what makes you feel out of spirits? There must be some cause. People do not shed tears only for the sake of shedding them, unless they are very perverse people and determined to be unhappy, and I hope you are not one of these."

Grace made no reply but fidgeted with her handkerchief. Miss Lee saw, however, that she was listening attentively and so continued in a playful tone.

"Come, let us see if we cannot find out what worries you, and when that is done, it will be easy to find a cure." And then speaking more seriously, she asked, "Do you know, my dear Grace, that numerous as the causes for sorrow may seem to you, they may all be traced to one source, and that is sin."

"Surely, Miss Lee," said Grace, roused by what seemed to her so singular a remark, "you do not mean to say that it is wrong or sinful to be sorry for misfortunes or for the death of our friends?

"No, Grace, I did not say anything like that. On the contrary, it would be sinful to be so much without natural affection as not to feel sorry for the death or the sufferings of those we love, and though we should seek to be submissive under them, we are not expected to feel indifferent to our own troubles. But, my dear, what was the cause of the entrance of death and of sorrow into the world?"

Grace was well enough read in the Scriptures to remember and answer readily, "'Death came by sin,' but," she added, "I cannot see what that has to do with my being dull or not feeling happy."

"Perhaps because you have not looked carefully at the subject," said Miss Lee gently. "You must allow that generally there are only two things that can make us unhappy; either something apart from ourselves, (such as the loss of property or the loss of friends by death or otherwise) or something within ourselves. I know you could tell me that bodily disease often depresses the spirits, but," she said smiling, as she looked on Grace's rosy cheek and bright eyes, "we will put that out of the question, as it does not apply to your case. Judge yourself then, Grace, whether you have any cause to lament any want of outward advantages or blessings. Look around you, see the superabundance of good things and think if, through all your life, you have had one thing to bear that deserves to be called trouble. Nay, have you not been exempt from some calamities, from which even wealth cannot always shield its possessor? I think you have never been called to part with those you love by death."

"You make me ashamed of my discontent," said Grace ingenuously, "and yet I cannot help it, though I know I ought to be thankful for all these things and happy and satisfied, yet still I am not happy."

"Then, my dear, if you allow that your sorrow does not proceed from any outward cause, you should seek it in yourself. Will you try to do so, and I shall help you?"

Grace hesitated. She was really interested in the conversation, and yet she shrank (she knew not why) from pursuing it. Not that she was entirely unaware of the drift of all Miss Lee's remarks, but she did not believe that they could be justly applied to herself. Like many an older and wiser person, she could believe and admit that human beings in general are sinners; but she could not by any means admit that *she herself* was a sinner; or if a glimpse of the real truth was ever forced on her mind, a thousand excuses readily presented themselves. "If I have some faults, I have many virtues — more, perhaps, than people who make more pretensions. Everybody has some weakness or infirmity of temper or disposition, and I have mine, I suppose; but I am sure, quite sure, that I am not so wicked as people who pretend to be religious, say everybody is." With such thoughts as these, she would stifle every conviction of truth; and if ever the idea of a future judgment with its dread solemnly entered her thoughts, she would strive to dismiss it with some reflection like this: "The Bible says God is merciful, and if we do the best we can, what more can be required of us? Besides, Jesus came into the world to die for sinners, and He will not let me perish, I am sure." She had forgotten that by denying herself to be a sinner she put herself out of the class of those for whom Christ died; but if she could but tranquilize her conscience for the moment, she cared little by what means it was done.

"You do not answer me, Grace," said Miss Lee, after a pause of several minutes. "You are surely not unwilling to take a little trouble for the sake of finding out and removing the cause of your sadness? Or are you displeased with my offer of assistance? If so, I will go away, for I would not on any account force myself upon your confidence."

"Oh no, Miss Lee, no, no," said Grace, for the first time in her life really earnest in her purpose. "If you will help me I will be glad and grateful; I will indeed try to overcome all my pride and examine my own motives."

"Will you, dear Grace?" said Miss Lee joyfully, "and may I help you? Well then, to begin, let me ask you to lay aside not only your pride but your prejudice, and before you refuse to believe anything I may say, look at it closely. Think over it. We need not be in haste. We will find many an hour like this, when we can sit alone and converse. But to begin, as I said, you agree that there is something in your own mind which causes you sorrow, do you not?"

"Yes," said Grace, "that is very often the case; but just now I felt unhappy because I fancied that no one loves me."

"And now you see it was only a fancy," said Miss Lee, laughing, "and as we are both too grave and too much in earnest to talk about an idle fancy itself, we will look at what causes it; what made you think no one loves you?"

"I think I am afraid," said Grace, now in her turn laughing. "It must have been because I felt that I did not deserve anybody's love; just then at least."

"And are you better at one time than you are at another?"

"Why certainly!" said Grace in surprise, and then blushing, she added, "surely you, above everybody else, need not ask such a question. Am not I at some times much more cross and troublesome than at others?"

"You take a very practical view of the subject," said the smiling Miss Lee, "but you do not take my question in quite the light I intended it. What I mean is, is your heart, your temper, or your disposition any better or holier at one time than another?"

"Why, I suppose it must be, or else why am I better behaved some days than others?"

"Because you meet with fewer events that test your temper on those days! For instance, you were very angry with Ellen this morning for upsetting the inkstand on your composition book, but would you have been less angry with her an hour before if she had done it, when you were quietly reading?"

"No," said Grace thoughtfully; "I see I should have been in just as violent a passion at one time as the other. But I do not see what all this proves."

"It proves, my love, that your unhappiness is caused by sin; for you, yourself, say you are out of spirits because you fancy no one loves you, and you think no one loves you because you do not deserve to be loved. Now if you allow you do not deserve it, you allow that you have done something wrong, and that wrong thing — whether great or little — is sin."

"Do not say 'sin,'" exclaimed Grace impatiently; "you talk as if every little fault was a great sin. I am sure that, if I am passionate, I soon get over it. People say I have a good heart, and I know I try, sometimes at least, to do right."

"If your heart is good, Grace, how can it bring forth even an angry thought? Much more those tempers of anger which you frequently indulge in? Can a good tree bring forth evil fruit or a sweet fountain send forth bitter water?"

Grace was silenced, and Miss Lee proceeded,

"Do not you remember Christ says, 'From out of the heart proceed evil thoughts," and, as I said, 'every tree is known by its fruits.' If the fruit of your heart is such as you agree it to be, must not the heart itself be evil?"

"But what good does all your arguing do me?" said Grace, who was beginning to feel irritated. "You said you wanted to make me feel happier, and instead of that you are trying to convince me that I am very wicked, but I do not believe it."

"It is indeed my most earnest wish to make you happier, Grace, and that is the reason I am trying to convince you of the sinfulness of your heart, that you may be induced to seek a new one."

Grace angrily withdrew her hand from Miss Lee's grasp, who was nearly at a loss how to proceed. She was unwilling to irritate Grace, and yet still more unwilling to lose this opportunity of impressing truth on her mind. After a moment's thought she said, "One more word, Grace, and then if you are tired or out of patience, I will be done. Do you not remember that Christ teaches us that if we indulge in angry thoughts, we transgress that

command which says, "Thou shalt do no murder"?
We transgress it in spirit at least, though God's
grace restrains us from committing the dreadful
act."

"And do you mean to say," said Grace (who
was surprised and startled by the solemn tone in
which the question had been asked) "that a
passionate person is, in the sight of God, as guilty as
a murderer?"

"No! oh! no! dear Grace, I only mean to say
he would be a murderer if God's grace did not
restrain him. I only wish you to see that it is no
merit in any one of us if we have not gone so far in
wickedness as some others. I wish you to see that
the 'root of bitterness' is in us all."

"Grace! Grace! Where are you?" It was little
Ellen's voice. "Oh! here you are. Mother wants
you to go with her; and she says Miss Lee, if you
are not occupied, she will be pleased to have your
company. We are all going out riding."

"Think, dear Grace, of what I have said,"
whispered Miss Lee as they ran upstairs to get their
bonnets; and Grace, though she made no reply,
resolved that she would think of it, but it was only
to find something that would refute Miss Lee's
arguments.

Miss Lee herself felt pleased that she had
succeeded in getting Grace to think on the subject;
yet there was mingled with her pleasure a half-
fearful thought that Mr. and Mrs. Raymond might

be displeased with her for speaking so openly to Grace. "However," she thought, "I was never told I must not talk to the children on these subjects, and I am sure it is my duty to try to influence them to choose the service of God. Oh, if I could succeed with Grace, surely, surely, with her energy and quickness, she would do much good in the world! As it is, if she is left to the unrestrained indulgence of her temper, she will be miserable; and what can restrain it but a power stronger than any she can find in herself! I will take courage, and as I have long determined, I will now ask Mr. Raymond's permission to form the children into a Sunday-school class at home, since he does not choose that they should go to the one at the church. I am sure he cannot object, for he said only last Sunday that they ought to have some regular instruction in public worship," and so resolving, her mind recovered some peace.

The same day, Miss Lee found an opportunity to make her request. It was always the custom for herself and the children to spend their evenings with Mr. and Mrs. Raymond when they were at home; and this evening, after the children had gone to bed, Mrs. Raymond made some observation on the extreme irritability Grace had displayed and lamented the violence of her temper.

"It is really time she learned to check it," said her husband. "I wish, Miss Lee, it were possible for you to communicate to her some of your mildness."

"Miss Lee does what she can," said Mrs. Raymond, (who had a sincere regard for her) "but it is not easy to teach a person who does not wish to learn."

"Nor do I think it in my power to communicate any such good to her," said Miss Lee timidly. "That must be sought for from the One who alone has power to influence the heart so that it shall incline to patience and humility, rather than to strife and discontent. God alone has power to confer such grace."

"I think it very possible for Grace to become amiable and good-tempered, if she pleases, without becoming a gloomy fanatic," said Mr. Raymond coldly. "It destroys all self-respect and self-reliance to teach that we cannot mend our own faults if we choose so to do."

"Grace has tried, I know, to restrain her temper," said Miss Lee, "and yet, I am sorry to say, after a few days, it always gains the mastery over her again."

"Because she did not persevere long enough to make the restraint a habit," said Mr. Raymond.

"But," asked Miss Lee, "does it not require some strength beyond ourselves to exhibit this perseverance?"

"I suppose to please her parents and to make herself feel happier are motives strong enough to induce perseverance," replied Mr. Raymond.

"But, as these motives have not hitherto proved strong enough to effect that object, would it not be right to try to furnish some more powerful one?" asked Miss Lee.

"And what stronger motive would you give her?"

"The desire to please God."

"I hope," said Mr. Raymond, "my children all desire to please God; but I do not approve of forcing that subject on them always."

"Nor do I," said Miss Lee, a little hurt at the implication she thought he meant to convey in the last remark. "And I carefully avoid that fault. Indeed, so carefully that I fear I have fallen into the opposite extreme and have been silent when I should have spoken."

"No one can say that Miss Lee does not do her duty in that respect," said Mrs. Raymond kindly, "for if her tongue is silent, her life speaks."

"My dear Miss Lee, do not for one moment suppose I referred to you in the remark I made," exclaimed Mr. Raymond, "though, to be frank, before I knew you as well as I do now, I had classed you among those people to whom I have a great aversion. I mean those who, professing to be religious, would teach that this world is only a gloomy wilderness where people are meant to be miserable and who would subdue all innocent mirth as sinful. I request you pardon me, for this misunderstanding."

"Most willingly," said Miss Lee, laughing, "but may I ask why, if this was your idea of me, you allowed me to enter into a situation in which I was so likely to influence your children?"

"Principally, because I feared falling into the opposite extreme you spoke of just now, and hiring someone who professed no religious opinions and would not influence them at all. I had heard you described as 'very pious,' and as all the 'very pious' people that had hitherto come under my notice seemed to me very gloomy, I had erred by classing you with them; so I must apologize for the liberty I take in making such personal remarks; only you must allow me to say that in the future I shall believe it possible to unite real cheerfulness with earnest piety."

"Say rather," said Miss Lee, with some emotion, "that real piety always produces true joy and cheerfulness, yes! But we have wandered far from the subject we were speaking of just now, and to return to it, I have a request to make —something I have long desired. And what you have just said leads me to hope you will grant it."

"I must first know what it is. Something relating to the children, I suppose?"

"Yes," replied Miss Lee, and then, in as few words as she could, she mentioned her desire to study the Bible with the children on Sundays and give them some religious instruction. "As I knew something of your opinions in regard to making religion a subject of conversation with them, I would not venture to commence a Bible-class without your permission."

"I am sorry you did not mention this before. I could have no possible objection to such a thing," said Mr. Raymond. And Miss Lee, pleased and relieved from her anxiety that she had been doing, in her conversation with Grace, what Mr. Raymond might disapprove, bade them goodnight and went to her own room.

The next morning she spoke to Mary and Grace of her plan and asked if they were willing. Mary assented with her usual promptness, which was just as often the result of indifference as of real humility; but Grace, though she did not refuse, was evidently not pleased with the proposal. Her conversation with Miss Lee had left a deep impression on her mind, but not the one her friend would have desired. So far from humbling her or making her feel her dependence on God, it had roused all the pride and opposition of her heart against the truth of her guilt and helplessness. She would not bow her heart to acknowledge that she was altogether evil and that, if left to herself, she would have become as bad as the worst criminal; and yet in her secret thoughts she could not resist the conviction. She felt miserable, depressed, and comfortless, and by no effort she made could she succeed in shaking off these feelings. Too proud to disclose the source of her unhappiness even to Miss

Lee, she avoided every one and for several days opposed every attempt Miss Lee made to converse with her. Even if she had been persuaded to speak, so agitated was her mind, she would have found great difficulty in deciding the cause of her uneasiness. "The light was shining in the darkness, and the darkness comprehended it not." She had never learned to bring her thoughts, her words, and her deeds to be examined in this light, that their evil might be "made manifest." Her rebellious heart struggled to shake off its convictions, but He who can bring good out of evil purposed that the very strength of her opposition should lead to actions that should convince her of her guilt and dependence on Him.

The more resolute and earnest she grew in her efforts to banish her tormenting thoughts and the more bitter and determined she became in her opposition to the truth, the more unhappy she felt, and as her unhappiness increased, her temper became more ungovernable. By turns she would be moody and silent or restless and passionate, and it required all Miss Lee's watchfulness and patience to prevent her from engaging in constant disputes with her sisters, who were both anxious to avoid her company. They declared, "Grace never in all her life had been so cross as she was now." For two or three weeks this continued, and each Sunday she contrived some excuse for absenting herself from the sitting-room during the time appointed for their

Bible-lessons, and Miss Lee's heart was saddened by seeing how little interest even Mary and Ellen seemed to take in them. "But," she whispered to herself on the third Sunday, (when Grace left the room, saying she had a headache) "I will still hope. To doubt and fear I will give no heed, for how know I which may thrive, the late or early sown?"

"How pretty! oh how pretty!" said little Ellen, as Grace one day (on returning from a walk) laid on the table a delicate little box made of mother-of-pearl; it was very thin, almost transparent, and carved in the most delicate manner. "Where did you get it, Grace? and what is it for?," pursued the child, attempting to take it in her hands.

"Mother just bought it for me. But do not touch it, Ellen; let it alone, I say, or you will let it fall and break it."

"Oh, I will not break it. Do just let me look at it," said Ellen, stretching her hand out for it, as Grace held it beyond her reach, and then, as her sister turned to answer a question of Mary's, she made a sudden lunge to seize the box; but failing to grasp it firmly, it slipped through her fingers and in a moment lay in fragments on the floor!

Grace was furious! Enraged by Ellen's carelessness and so without stopping to think of the consequences, Grace grasped her arm and shook her violently with all her strength and then flung the child from her, who, falling with her head against the sharp corner of a mahogany foot-stool, was completely stunned and lay motionless!

"What! oh what have I done! She is dead!" screamed Grace, when, after one moment of agonizing terror, she started forward to look at the face of the child who was now in Miss Lee's arms. "Oh, she is dead, she is dead, and I killed her!"

"Hush! hush! dear Grace," said Miss Lee, who, though as pale and as frightened, still retained her presence of mind. "I hope — I think — she is only stunned. Ring the bell and run quick and bring some water."

Grace tried to obey but, too much overcome with terror to walk, sank on her knees and with clasped hands gazed earnestly on the rigid, white face of the child. Mary, however, was more calm, and the loud peal that she gave the bell, in a few moments summoned assistance, and Ellen was carried to bed. Even before her mother had been informed of the accident, she began to revive.

When the child had been carried from the room, every one except Grace followed. Horror at the result of her violence deprived her of all strength. She believed for the moment that Ellen was really dead! Utterly frightened and dismayed, she remained on her knees with her face buried in her hands, unable to speak, to think, or even to weep. A dull, hopeless, yet agonizing feeling of despair filled her mind, and but one dim idea could find a place, "Oh, that I might die too!

"But then, where, oh, where should I go? What would become of me? Can I ever forget, can I ever fly from the recollection of what I have done?"

"Indeed, indeed, Grace, she is better," said Miss Lee, running into the room and deeply moved by the expression of agony and despair in Grace's features; "we even hope she is not seriously hurt."

"How can I ever," — she tried to go on, but she was choked with mingled emotions of joy and terror; and Miss Lee, who hoped such a flood of tears would soothe her agitation better than any thing she could say, did not check them nor even attempt to sympathize with her beyond a gentle pressure of the hand.

The injury that little Ellen had received proved on examination to be quite trifling compared with their fears; and the physician assured them that in two or three days every trace of the accident would probably disappear; but it seemed to Grace that she could never recover a feeling of tranquility, and that the recollection of her agony would haunt her all her life long.

Though all the family were perfectly aware of the cause of the accident, no one had the heart to utter a word of reproof, for the anguish Grace had endured was thought to be a sufficient punishment, and the kind tone in which every one addressed her contributed still further to soften and subdue her. For several hours she could not summon resolution to go and see Ellen, although she longed to be assured, beyond all doubt, that she was really as much better as they had said. So it was not until an entreating message from Ellen herself was brought to her, that she could be persuaded even to go near the room where she was.

"Dear sister! Mother says you are so sorry you hurt me. I wanted to tell you I am not at all angry," exclaimed the child as Grace, bending over her, pressed her quivering lips to her check.

"Forgive me, dear sister! oh, say you forgive me, though I can never forgive myself."

"I am not at all angry, Grace. You would not have pushed me down if I had not been rude and snatched your box away. I am so sorry I broke it, sister."

"Don't speak of that, what does it matter now? And besides, have not I, a thousand times, been more unjust and unkind to you?"

"Say no more now, Grace," whispered her mother. "You only make yourself more unhappy and disturb Ellen. Let her go to sleep if she will."

The unhappy Grace now sought in solitude an opportunity to freely vent her aroused convictions. Shutting herself up in her own room, she knelt down and tried to give thanks to God for averting the dreadful harm she had at first imagined and to implore pardon for the passion that had led to it; but every attempt she made to form her thoughts into words was vain. It seemed as if now, for the first time, she could realize the magnitude of her wickedness. It was not so much the events of this day as the conviction of the sinfulness of her heart, which distressed her. The recollection of her conversation with Miss Lee some weeks before flashed across her mind, and she exclaimed aloud, "You were right, Miss Lee. My heart is indeed evil, desperately wicked; how, oh, how can it be forgiven? Where shall I get a new one?"

Part Two

People of the living God
I have sought the world around,
Paths of sin and sorrow trod,
Peace and comfort nowhere found.
Now to you my spirit turns –
Turns a fugitive, unblest;
Brethren, where your altar burns,
Oh! receive me into rest.
                    ~James Montgomery

Grace dared not pray. How could God listen to so great a sinner? How could she even dare to ask Him? Thus she thought, but there she was on her knees in trembling and speechless distress, (not even weeping) even she knew not how long. The heart cannot for any length of time endure such violent emotions; and gradually the excitement gave place to a feeling of numbness and despair.

She left her room and mingled with the family, but she walked as in a dream and only answered mechanically the questions addressed to her. Every one noticed that she was still much depressed, but they attributed it altogether to her regret for the injury to Ellen, and her father begged her to go early to bed, as he thought she needed rest and would become ill if she was allowed to brood over her regrets so much. Quite indifferent to what place she might be in, she willingly complied, and Mary (who slept with her) accompanied her, and in a few minutes after she had laid her head on the pillow, she was in a profound sleep.

Not so Grace. As she lay in the dark and silent chamber, she recalled one by one the incidents of the day, and then looking carefully back over her past life, her memory brought up incident after incident, sin after sin, till her feelings of agonizing distress revived. She lay and listened to the sounds of the household until they died away one by one, and all seemed at rest, and she could contain herself no longer.

"I must, I must have some relief. I cannot pray for myself. I will go and ask Miss Lee to pray for me. God will hear her; yes, surely He will hear one so good as she is," she thought, and slipping from the bed so as not to disturb Mary, she softly opened the door of Miss Lee's room, which adjoined theirs.

It was not so late as Grace had thought, and Miss Lee had only a short time before retired to her chamber and was not yet prepared for rest. She was standing by her dressing-table, leaning over a Bible that lay open before her. She started and turned around at the sound of the opening door, and Grace saw that her face was streaming with tears.

"Why are you not asleep, Grace, my love?" she asked in surprise. "Are you sick? or what is the matter?"

"I cannot sleep — I cannot rest. Oh! I feel as if there was no more rest, no more peace for me while I live; and when I die, Miss Lee, what will become of me?" and she wept bitterly.

"Father, a weary heart hath come to Thee for peace," thought Miss Lee within herself, as she folded Grace in her arms; but for a moment or two she could not speak. Though she had hoped — prayed — believed the events of the day would make an impression on her, she had not expected it would be so soon manifested. Miss Lee was quite unprepared for this overwhelming and sudden sense of her misery which Grace now expressed. Had she been aware how long and how resolutely Grace had been struggling to resist the convictions of her sinfulness, perhaps she could have better accounted for the violence of her emotion, now that these convictions had been brought home with such irresistible force. In proportion now to the strength of her resistance and pride and self-righteousness was the depth of her humiliation and self-abasement. Can the hands of man be strong, or can their hearts endure when the Spirit of God enters into judgment with them?

"I am so wretched, Miss Lee! I am so miserable," said Grace at length, as she raised her head. "Do you remember what you told me, 'That allowing anger to have dominion over one is to have the spirit of a murderer.' I feel that, now I know it. Such a spirit is in me! and how can God ever pardon me? If even I can see and feel how wicked my nature is, what must I be in His sight?" and she again covered her face with her hands.

"But do not you remember what I told you at the same time? That God's grace restrains us from the extremity of our wickedness. And has He not this day even prevented the most fatal effect of your violent temper? If He could, even while you were so sinfully yielding to your evil temper, mercifully prevent the most dreadful result which you fear; think you that this mercy is any less towards you now that you acknowledge your sin and grieve for it?" inquired Miss Lee. "For Christ's sake, His saving, as well as His restraining, grace will be given you. Oh, believe that there is mercy in Christ for the vilest sinner."

"Not for me! There is no peace, no mercy for me. God can never forgive me if He is just. My very prayers must have been hateful to Him. Never in my whole life have I done one good deed in His sight or thought one good thought. How can the just God forgive one like me?"

"Christ came to seek and to save them that are lost; yes, it was even for such He died — even for such that He now lives to make intercession. Believe in Him. Ask God's mercy in Christ's name, and you shall receive it," replied Miss Lee.

"I cannot believe. I know not how; and even if I would, He would not receive me. I have neglected Him and cast Him aside and refused to hear Him, and now He will refuse to hear me."

"Do not thus measure the mercy of God in Christ. Consider what He Himself says," urged Miss Lee, opening her Bible. "He is merciful and gracious, slow to anger, and willing to save to the uttermost all those who come unto Him. Are not you willing to go to Him, Grace?"

"Yes," replied Grace, "if I knew how to go. But I do not know what to say or how to say it."

"Can you not say, 'God be merciful to me a sinner'? Do you not feel that you are a sinner? Do you not wish for mercy?"

"Yes; but when I would say it, I think how can God be merciful to me? How can He, who is so just, withhold punishment from me?" replied Grace with deep feeling.

""Because you do not remember that Christ has died that we may be saved. He has already borne our sins in His own Body, on the cross. Ask in His name, plead His sacrifice, ask in faith, and He will hear and forgive, and it shall be unto you according to your desire."

"But my heart, Miss Lee, is so very wicked that I am sure if God forgives me now, I shall only go and sin again, and I do not know how to believe in Christ in the way you tell me nor even how to try."

"Pray, then, 'Lord, I believe! Help Thou my unbelief!' If your trust is in Him, He will never leave you nor forsake you. Whom He justifies, them He also sanctifies."

"Pray for me, Miss Lee, pray for me," pleaded Grace. "I cannot pray for myself. Pray that God will give me the blessings you have spoken of."

And with all the earnestness and faith of a truly Christian heart did Miss Lee implore the mercy of God on the broken-hearted, penitent child. She prayed that she might be saved from unbelief and despair; that she might not so undervalue the sufferings and death of the Redeemer as to suppose His atonement was not sufficient to purchase pardon for even the most guilty; that she might trust in the blood that was shed, for the forgiveness of her sins; that she might have grace even now to believe and obey the gospel; that the Sun of Righteousness might arise and shine on her darkness and heal the broken heart and give peace to the troubled, contrite spirit.

And so it was, that while she prayed, a sweet calm stole over the heart of Grace. The sense of her sinfulness was not lessened, but she could see that the mercy of God in Christ — His grace — His love —could much more abound than her own sins. At first, the possibility, then the certainty of pardon and acceptance from God dawned on her, and a child-like, submissive feeling took the place of despondency, so that she could say, "Abba, Father," in the spirit of adoption, confessing with brokenness, "Thou, O God, art merciful above all that we are able to ask or think."

The night was far advanced, and Miss Lee and her transformed young friend returned to their rooms. The former could not sleep until she had once more knelt and poured out some expression of the gratitude and praise that filled her heart. "Never again," she thought, "will I for one moment doubt that God will hear and answer the weakest prayer that is offered in faith. Never will I permit myself to feel discouraged because He seems to withhold an answer. Dear Grace! What a happy life thine may now be! She only needed sweetness of temper and pious tastes to make her a most delightful companion, and I have no fear but that the seeds of such a taste are now planted in her mind. Oh, may they bear fruit abundantly to the praise of divine grace!"

Grace was exhausted with the excitement of the past day, wearied with the many and varied emotions she had undergone, and gradually sleep overcame her. When at an unusually late hour she awoke from her slumbers, the blessed, certain truth, that she was a "new creature" flashed across her mind, and casting herself upon her knees, she offered up her first sacrifice of humble, fervent prayer and grateful, adoring praise to Him who had ransomed her from sin. Then she hastened to Miss

Lee's room to share her new-born happiness, and to ascertain how little Ellen was.

Miss Lee had already been to inquire and was delighted to be able to tell Grace that the child seemed quite recovered and perfectly free from all mark of injury, except a bruise upon the place that had struck the stool; and she then affectionately inquired of Grace what her own feelings were.

"Happy, Miss Lee! oh, how happy!" replied Grace. "And to think that such happiness should be bestowed on one so undeserving!"

"Remember, my dear, for whose sake it has been given and strive to prove your gratitude by obeying His command."

"I will try, and you must teach me how — will you not?"

"Most gladly, Grace, will I strive to teach you all in my power; but your Bible will be your best teacher. If you study that with the determination to obey its precepts and ask God to give the Holy Spirit to enlighten you, you cannot fail of obtaining all the instruction and all the strength you need."

"I feel as if I could never forgive myself for having so long neglected and despised God's holy word," said Grace; "for though it is true I often read it and thought some parts of it beautiful, now I know He did not give it to us merely to be admired by our minds, but to purify our lives, to make us understand His holy purposes towards us, and to lead us to submit to them. I think if we do not take the Bible in the way He meant it to be taken, it would be better for us that we had never seen it."

"Yes, my dear," said Miss Lee, as she turned over the pages of her own Bible and inserted a few slips of paper in them; "but we have not time to talk now, as it is near breakfast, and I would ask you to read and study the chapters I have here marked before we converse further. One word more, Grace," she said as she was about to leave the room. "You are, of course, aware that it is but right that your parents should know of the change which has taken place in your feelings. It is better that it should be know to them at once. Will you tell them, or shall I?"

"If you will, dear Miss Lee, I shall be most grateful," said Grace; "but you do not think they will be displeased? Father does not like people to be what he calls 'too religious.' But it will take all my life, all my powers of mind and body, to show how good God has been to me."

"I hope, dear Grace," said Miss Lee hesitatingly, "that Mr. Raymond will not show much displeasure, especially when I tell him how unhappy you were; but if he should, it will be your duty to try to reconcile him to it by the most dutiful submission in all other things and by striving to make the doctrines of the gospel seem lovely by exemplifying them in your daily life and conduct. However he may feel about the change, he cannot but be pleased with the fruits of it, if they appear in your meekness, gentleness, and readiness to give up self for the sake of making others happy."

"I had not thought of this before, Miss Lee," said Grace sadly. "I do not know how I could bear to have them displeased with me for this."

"My dear girl," replied Miss Lee, "you must not expect that because you have now submitted to the yoke of Christ, you will be wholly free from trouble. He invariably gives to each of His people some cross which they must take up and bear; but, if we meekly submit and patiently endure it, He also gives us strength and assists us under the burden. Possibly the displeasure of your parents is a trial whereby He means to prove your faith, to see if you love Him better even than you love them; and if you bear this trial patiently, you will soon find that your patience will produce experience, and experience a more firm hope and an assurance of the possession of the love of God."

Miss Lee sought the earliest opportunity after breakfast of informing Mr. and Mrs. Raymond of all that had passed between herself and Grace. She described Grace's alarm and terror when she thought Ellen was dead and placed in the strongest light the state in which her mind had been on the proceeding night; how overwhelmed with despair and agony; and the arguments and means she herself had used for calming it; the evident relief Grace had received, and the resolution she professed of giving herself wholly to God and striving to continue in

His service. It was not without much anxiety that Miss Lee explained these matters, for she was aware that Mr. Raymond would attribute only to her influence all that might displease them. So, although she knew she had only done her duty and encouraged herself by that recollection, she still shrank from meeting the explosion of violent feeling with which she feared Mr. Raymond would greet her communication. But though he heard her with a frowning face and showed in his manner that he was excessively displeased, he did not at first say one word. Not so his wife.

"This is too bad!" she exclaimed. "Grace seems intended for the torment of my life! It was bad enough to have to put up with her fits of passion; but it will be infinitely worse to have her turn a fanatic. I know well if she once takes a fancy of the kind into her head she will follow it to the extreme point — she is so headstrong and self-willed."

"Yes," said her husband, "that is just what I fear. Grace's enthusiasm will, if this subject once interests her, make her a perfect fanatic."

"I hope," said Miss Lee mildly, "that you will find yourselves mistaken. I trust she will show that the change in her temper and conduct are quite improved."

"I have no desire to speak with her on the subject," replied Mrs. Raymond angrily; "my only hope is that she will keep out of my sight as much as possible, till she comes to her senses as I expect she will after she has made herself ridiculous for a while."

Miss Lee did not reply. She was distressed more on Grace's account than her own to see how bitter their opposition was; and she tried to give as little fuel to its fire as possible by avoiding even a seeming contradiction. Her forbearance had but little effect; however, as Mrs. Raymond continued to speak in the same strain for some time, until Miss Lee, thinking she had done all in her power to soothe her feelings, retired.

"What is to be done?" asked Mrs. Raymond, when she had left the room; "do you think it right to allow her to continue with the children?"

"What else can we do now?" replied her husband; "even should she leave, it will not undo the mischief. Would it not rather raise a spirit of opposition in Grace, and make her more determined in her folly? Besides, if we parted with Miss Lee, where would we find any one so exceptional as she is in all points, save this?"

"I am afraid you are right," replied the wife, "but what shall we do? Sit quietly down and let Grace hide all her fine talents, her wit, her beauty from the world and spend all her time in running about to prayer meetings, missionary meetings, sewing societies, and every other society that a fanatical spirit has called into existence? We shall have her, I suppose, teaching a class of dirty children in the Sunday-school, like Margaret Ridley. And, by and by, when she is a few years older, refusing some grand match because the gentleman is not 'pious'; and marrying a missionary with as little money as brains, like Lucy Preston." So she ran on, till overcome by the picture of her own fancy had conjured up, she put her handkerchief to her eyes and fairly wept.

"Come, come, Julia," replied Mr. Raymond, "let us hope she will not go to quite such extremes as those. She is very young, very lively, and very fond of pleasure. We will take her out a good deal. She shall go to the play and see company; and these foolish fancies that are probably the result of her excited imagination will fade away. Don't let us make any fuss, but just behave as if this had not been; and my word for it, we will, in a month or two, (perhaps sooner) see the last of Grace's new notions." And so saying, he took his hat and departed to his counting-house. Mrs. Raymond, after paying a visit to little Ellen, soon lost the memory of her vexation in the pages of the last fashionable novel.

Miss Lee was too prudent to tell Grace all that had passed between herself and Mr. and Mrs. Raymond, but she deemed it right to tell her at least enough to prepare her for reproach and opposition. Grace received the news quite as meekly as her friend had hoped, and though she shed a few tears, they were soon wiped away, and her mind recovered its former peace. Her sisters did not show much surprise at her present meekness and submission, as they supposed it was caused by the accident of the previous day, and the only notice taken of it was by little Ellen, who declared to her nurse, that she would be willing to bump her head every day, if it would make Grace always half as good-natured as she was now!

During their hours for study, Grace strove by the greatest deference and respect to manifest her gratitude and love to Miss Lee; and though her mind was so preoccupied by her newfound happiness to pay as much attention as usual to her lessons as she ought, she tried to do so for the sake of pleasing her teacher. Both were glad when the duties of the morning were over, and they could retire to Miss Lee's room to converse in freedom.

Grace had employed the time, while Miss Lee was occupied with her parents, in examining the Bible chapters marked for her. These she found to be the fifty-first Psalm, the sixth chapter of the epistle to the Romans, and the second and third chapters of the first epistle of John. And she rose from the reading with the resolution to seek a still deeper humiliation of spirit — a still more contrite heart; to show that she was dead unto sin but alive unto God in Christ, by striving to mortify the deeds of the flesh; and to prove her gratitude to Him who had been the propitiation of her sin by loving all "in deed and in truth" for whom He had died.

"How pleasant it will be," said Grace joyfully, as she closed the door of Miss Lee's room and drew her chair close to her friend's, "for us to sit here and converse. I expect to pass many happy hours with you here, Miss Lee. I love now to talk of and listen to the things you love best."

"I hope we shall often have these pleasant discussions, dear," responded her friend; "but we must not be too sure it will last." And Miss Lee sighed as she thought how improbable it was that she would be allowed to remain in her present situation, while the influence she exerted over Grace was regarded as so very undesirable. She was now as anxious to stay as she had been before to leave; and it saddened her to think of departing just when the circumstances had made it so pleasant to remain.

"Do not talk so," replied Grace affectionately; "I do not see anything that is likely to separate us for some time at least; and do not let us overcloud that time by talking of parting."

"Many circumstances might contribute soon to separate us, my love," replied Miss Lee, (who, though she did not think it necessary to communicate her fears to Grace, wished to prepare her for the event of a separation) "and I hope, even if I leave you, you would still be very happy. There is no happiness to the Christian like communion with God; and that happiness, dear Grace, is always open to you."

"But I am so weak, so ignorant. O Miss Lee! I should never be able to go forward at all by myself."

"Let me warn you, Grace," said Miss Lee with deep seriousness, "from the very first, to avoid the error of depending on any human being for support and strength. The very best human being is but a broken reed and if you lean on such, it will break and may pierce you with many arrows."

"What shall I do then?"

"Trust wholly in God. Ask Him, and He will give you grace to help in time of need. Depend on Him for instruction, and in all times of perplexity, He will guide you. You shall hear a voice saying, "This is the way, walk ye in it." O Grace, it is those who look wholly to God for strength who alone are really strong, who alone drink deeply of the cup of salvation."

"But Miss Lee, are we not to receive and try to profit by the sermons we hear, the books we read, and the conversation of pious friends?"

"Certainly, my dear, but we are to take these as entirely subordinate to the teaching of God, because if unaccompanied by His Spirit, they are utterly without effect, and we must be willing to dispense with them if He sees fit to withdraw them from us."

"Miss Lee," said Grace, after a pause of a few minutes, "I think I should love to profess myself a Christian and share in all means God has appointed for the good of His people. Do you think Father and Mother will allow it?"

"I fear, my love, they would object," answered Miss Lee. "But I do not think that need be any cause of anxiety to you at present. It is perhaps too soon for you to think of such a step."

"Too soon!" repeated Grace in a surprised and disappointed tone. "I did not think you would have thought that. I supposed it was right for every one who feels as I do to wish to share in all the privileges of Christians."

"It is right to wish for those privileges and to look forward to partaking of them. Every true Christian naturally desires publicly to profess his love to the Saviour and his desire and determination to be devoted to His service, but we must not be too hasty in so doing. Jesus commands us to 'count the cost' before we resolve to follow Him."

"I have resolved. I have determined, Miss Lee. Do not try to discourage me now or make me think my resolutions will come to nothing," exclaimed Grace.

"Not for the world, Grace, would I do so," replied Miss Lee. "If I speak thus, it is only to lead you to make firmer resolves and to pray more earnestly for strength to keep them. Recollect that you are very young — almost a child in age — and oh! Grace, you do not yet know the strength of the temptations you may meet with! Many have professed themselves followers of Christ, who, after a brief time, have proved by their lives that they never knew Him, nor He them, and whose conduct has brought disgrace upon religion. Watch and pray — try yourself; be very sure you are a Christian before you profess and call yourself one."

"I supposed," said Grace, (who was deeply impressed by the solemn earnestness with which Miss Lee spoke) "that we ought at once to take our stand on the side of Christ, as soon as we felt the power of His religion."

"Assuredly so," replied Miss Lee. "The Bible everywhere shows a serious call to duty. It says to repent, believe, and be submissive to the will of God, but it also teaches us that following Christ does not consist of mere ordinances. Though these are very often the means of much benefit, they are but a means. Dear Grace, do not depend on them very much. Try, rather, to show you are a Christian by your every-day life than by an outward profession. At least, let the sincerity of your repentance and faith be tested by time before you publicly join yourself to the church."

Like all people of ardent temperament, Grace was too eager and too impatient. She longed to press forward without stopping to consider if her strength would enable her to maintain the pace. She knew not yet that the Christian path is "like the shining light that shineth more and more unto the perfect day."

"Set out in the cool of the day and travel at a pace, and you will probably be able to continue through the day," says one. "I have seen those who drove much too fast at first and were not able to continue their journey," says another, whose experience had guided and guarded many a soul in the paths of a godly life. It was this mistake from which Miss Lee sought to guard Grace. Though she well knew that Christ is able to keep that which has been committed to Him safe until the final day, she was also aware that Grace's comfort and happiness would be lessened in the meanwhile, if from aiming at what was, at present, beyond her strength, she should for a while fall away. Besides, though she trusted that Grace's heart was really changed, nothing but time and trials could prove it, for the heart is "deceitful above all things."

Grace acquiesced in her teacher's reasonings. She now distrusted herself too much to suppose that she was too competent to judge in the matter and meekly listened to Miss Lee's cautions to be especially watchful over her temper. "Do not suppose, Grace," she said, "because you hope you are now a 'new creature' in Christ Jesus, that you are so safe that you need give yourself no further concern. No! be assured that if you give way to carelessness, you are none of His. Do you remember what our pastor said: 'The power and grace of Christ are not so put forth as to dispense with diligence in the exercise of every duty but to secure the exercise of such diligence,' and in fact this is the only rule by which we can judge ourselves."

It was not long before Grace had an opportunity of testing her new principles. Attached to her father's house was a large garden; and a plot of ground had been assigned to each of the children and was called theirs. Though Mary was too indolent and Ellen too volatile to pay much attention to those assigned to them, with Grace it was entirely different. Always very active and persevering, she was delighted at being at full liberty to plan and arrange, labour and watch the effects of her work; and the gardener declared that Miss Grace beat him completely. For, though he gave her just the same roots and seeds which he planted elsewhere, her plants would always be finer, and her flowers would smell sweeter than any he raised. If there was some flattery in this, there was also much truth. Grace's labours were certainly well rewarded; and this summer she had been even more successful than usual. A present of some rare and extremely beautiful plants, in pots, had been given to her; and to tend these, to water them, to place them in the sun, and to watch day by day the appearance of numerous buds had been her especial delight. Several of them were now on the very point of blooming, and Grace was watching anxiously for the opening of the most rare and lovely of them all, from which she wished to make a drawing to present to her mother. For greater convenience in moving them, she had placed them on a small and very light stand; and this she had drawn to the edge of the walk on the day before this blossom was expected to expand in order to remove them from the shade of a neighbouring tree.

"I think, Mary, it will certainly be quite open by this time to-morrow," Grace said, as she stood with her sister, examining the rapid progress it had made. "Only see what a perfect purple appears through the green sheath! It will certainly more than compensate for all my care and pains," she continued, with the well-deserved satisfaction of one who had toiled hard and waited for a just reward.

"Yes," answered Mary, "I almost wish, Grace, that I had accepted Father's offer to give me some of those roots. I really do love flowers, but it is so much trouble to take care of them. However, you seem likely to be repaid for all your trouble."

"Yes," said Grace, "more than repaid"; and as she turned suddenly, she cried, "Be careful! —oh, be careful!" for the heedless little Ellen was now flying down the path on her tricycle. "You will run against my stand!"

The warning came too late! In attempting to avoid her sisters, who had drawn back to the opposite side of the path, Ellen crashed full against the stand with such force that she not only overturned it, but, unable to stop the tricycle, she ran over and destroyed several of the plants that fell in her path; and among them, the beautiful shrub in which Grace had taken such pride! The wheel of the tricycle passed over the half-opened flower, destroying not only it, but any hope that it might be restored!

The blood rushed to Grace's face, and with an angry exclamation, she started forward, her upraised hand ready to strike the child, who, aghast at the mischief she had done, was now standing motionless, looking on the ruined plants. For one moment she stood with her hand thus suspended over Ellen; and then, struggling to suppress her violent emotions, with a half-uttered cry to her heavenly Father for help, she hid her face in her handkerchief, sat down on the overturned stand, and sobbed aloud. But it was as much in gratitude that she had been saved from the indulgence of her temper as for grief at her disappointment. Mary and Ellen, astonished equally by Grace's forbearance, stood by in speechless wonder for some minutes, till at length Ellen ventured to put her arm around Grace's neck and whisper:

"I am so sorry, Grace! I am really very sorry, dear sister. Don't cry, and I will give you any thing I have — all my pretty things, to make up for it. I'll give you my beautiful new work-box and the pictorial book that Father bought me yesterday"; and she sighed, pained with regrets at the magnitude of the sacrifice she was making.

"No," said Grace, as soon as she could find her voice. "You need not give me any thing, Ellen. I can easily forgive you"; and the tears started afresh, as she looked around and saw how entire was the wreck of her garden hopes. Hardly one plant remained unbroken; and one half of the garden bed itself was cut up by the tricycle, which lay overturned in the middle.

"How different Grace is now," whispered Ellen to Mary. "I wonder what has made her so the last few days."

Grace knew the change in her conduct was noticed and talked about by the children. This did not bring her to vanity, but rather shame for her past. And while her heart was filled with gratitude for being restrained from violence towards her sister, she longed to be alone, that she might confess and bewail the hasty words and passionate feeling to which she had yielded; so, taking the first opportunity of leaving them, she retired to her own room to kneel in repentant prayer for more watchfulness over herself and for new strength to resist her besetting sin.

"Do not be discouraged," said Miss Lee, when Grace came to her with many tears and confessing her failing. "It is not by one effort we can expect to subdue a fault that has so long been gathering strength from indulgence. Victory is promised as we continue in well-doing. Rather let every failure incite you to fresh and more vigorous efforts. I met with a beautiful remark the other day, the substance of which was, 'If our Saviour commands us to forgive our brethren, not seven times, but seventy times seven, what measure or limit can we put to His forgiveness whose thoughts and ways are as far above ours as the heavens are above the earth?' "

"That was indeed beautiful," said Grace; "but can I never hope to be completely freed from this sin? Can I never be quite sure that I am out of all danger of yielding to it?"

"God's grace is sufficient for us. I suppose that our complete deadness to sin and freedom from the assaults of the tempter are part of the happiness reserved for us in heaven. If, however, we are steadfast in the faith, we shall go on from strength to strength, till we arrive at last in the blissful presence of our blessed Saviour, to receive the crowning token of His grace and to be holy as He is holy, and dwell with Him for ever."

"I see by the paper," said Mr. Raymond, a few days after the accident in the garden, when they were sitting at breakfast, "that the troupe of Viennese dancers will be here in a day or two; so, Julia, I will take you and the children to see them. I suppose it will be of no use to invite you, Miss Lee," he said with a smile.

"It would certainly be unnecessary," answered Miss Lee, "as, even if my views of duty allowed me to go, my health would not."

"You cannot plead such an excuse, Grace," said her father with an arch smile; "so I shall secure five seats. I suppose even you, Miss Malapert, would like to see little girls no bigger than yourself go flying about in the air," as he pinched the cheek of little Ellen who sat beside him.

"If you please, Father, do not take a seat for me," said Grace timidly; (for it was the first time she had been called on to run counter to her parents' wishes) "I have no wish to go."

"Why not?" inquired her father. "You were always pleased when I proposed any thing of the kind before."

"I have no wish to go to such a place now. I do not think of it as I formerly did," said Grace respectfully, her eyes falling beneath her father's penetrating look.

"Tut, tut, child! If you have no better reason to give than that, you had better go. Your old taste will revive when you get there."

"I do not want it to revive, my dear Father. I do not think I ought to go, and I must ask you to please let me stay at home." Thus she pleaded, and her eyes filled with tears.

"You don't think it right to go!" said Mr. Raymond, mimicking her tone; for he was losing his temper. "And pray, Miss, who made you a judge over your parents? If I think it right, what business have you to object?"

Grace could only answer by her tears. Her father had never spoken to her in this tone before, and she did not know how to answer him without seeming disrespectful. Miss Lee, who sympathized with her distress, longed to say something to relieve it; but did not dare to speak, for fear of further irritating Mr. Raymond, who, after a few moments of awkward silence, said —

"Either stop crying, Grace, or leave the room." And then, as she rose from the table to go, he added, "Since you do not choose to go, I will not force you. But, understand me — if you separate yourself from the family in one pleasure, you may in all; for one amusement I offer to you is just as innocent as another."

This was a hard trial to Grace. She had, of course, lost all relish for such a scene as the theatre would present; but it was very painful to oppose her father's wishes and to seem to contradict and condemn as wrong what he asserted to be right, and to seem to treat with disrespect and ingratitude an offer made apparently with the sincerest desire to give her pleasure; and she shed many bitter tears when she had seated herself at her own window.

"Do not cry, Grace," said Miss Lee, who had followed her as soon as possible. "It is of no use; and you could not have done otherwise than you did. I expected you would meet with some such trial before long; and I rejoice that you have been able to endure it so well."

"I am thankful I had strength to be firm," said Grace. "But, oh! Miss Lee, it is so hard to bear Father's angry tone. He never spoke so to me before."

"My dear Grace, you must expect and prepare yourself to suffer for well-doing, 'for the servant is not above his master, nor the disciple above his Lord'; and did not even our Saviour receive reproaches and contempt, instead of praise, for the blessed works He did? Be tranquil, then, go steadily on and quench the unkindness with meekness; overcome evil with good."

And Grace did go steadily on. Daily did she seek for strength and wisdom from above by humble, fervent prayer; and God was exceedingly gracious to the voice of her cry, and exceedingly rich was the reward she received; for every act of self-denial, every effort she made to overcome her temper was blessed almost beyond her hopes; and every victory gained over it made the next easier.

Mr. Raymond was too indulgent and kindhearted to persist long in excluding Grace from any of the pleasures of which she felt at liberty to partake, and she was soon permitted to join in the daily rides and walks of her mother and sisters. Nay, so completely did she overcome them by her meekness that they acknowledged that she really was more agreeable now than when she had been such a little fury. Her religion, they all agreed, made the family much more happy in every respect.

At a proper time, Grace was permitted to declare her love to Christ in a public profession of her faith in Him as the only Saviour of sinners. She became a communicant in the church where she had from her childhood attended public worship; and the pastor, who had long lamented the indifference of the Raymond family to the calls of the gospel, hailed Grace's conversion as a "first-fruits" of a good work of grace and hoped that, through her, the rest of the family might be drawn into the fold of the Great Shepherd.

We leave our young friend at the threshold of the strait and narrow path that leads to life. The same grace that enabled her to see her lost and helpless state, and that led her to embrace the hope set before her in the gospel, proved sufficient to give her an early and complete victory over strong temptations. The same grace is promised to every child of God and will be bestowed in answer to believing prayer in such forms and degrees as shall most perfectly promote the glory of God and the salvation and eternal life of the soul.